For Sam and Blake for planting the seed.
And for anyone who needs a personal time out now and then.

Text and illustrations copyright © 2018 Barney Saltzberg
Cover and internal design by Simon Stahl

CIP data for this book is available from the Library of Congress.

Published by Creston Books, LLC
www.crestonbooks.co

ISBN 978-1-939547-42-2
Source of Production: 1010 Printing
Printed and bound in China
5 4 3 2 1

Enough
IS
ENOUGH!

Barney Saltzberg

Creston Books

Will had pushed Olive out of her
chair more times than she could count.

"Enough is enough!" said Olive.

"How do you know when enough is enough?" asked Will.

"I just know," said Olive.

"I haven't had enough," said Will.
"I want to play with you."

"I want to be alone for a while," said Olive.

"Being alone sounds lonely," said Will.

"It sounds wonderful to me," said Olive.

"You forgot your book," said Will.

"Maybe you could read it while we are both having some alone time," said Olive.

"Did you forget that I can't read?" said Will.

"Just look at the pictures," said Olive. "I will read the book to you when I come back."

"I need some space..."

"...and time."

It was very quiet, being away from Will.

Almost too quiet.

"Now I'm ready!" said Olive.

"Me, too," said Will.

"Enough is enough!" said Olive.

And it was.